WHOOO'S
Haunting the Teeny Tiny Ghost?

by **Kay Winters**

illustrated by **Lynn Munsinger**

HarperCollinsPublishers

To Nancy Larrick Crosby,
my teacher, mentor, and friend
—K.W.

The art for this book was created in pen and ink and watercolors.

Whooo's Haunting the Teeny Tiny Ghost?
Text copyright © 1999 by Kay Winters
Illustrations copyright © 1999 by Lynn Munsinger
Printed in the U.S.A. All rights reserved.
Visit our web site at http://www.harperchildrens.com.

Library of Congress Cataloging-in-Publication Data
Winters, Kay.
    Whooo's haunting the teeny tiny ghost? / by Kay Winters ; illustrated by Lynn
Munsinger.
        p.   cm.
    Summary: The teeny, tiny, very timid ghost tries to be brave when he suspects that his
house is haunted.
    ISBN 0-06-027358-5. — ISBN 0-06-027359-3 (lib. bdg.)
    [1. Ghosts—Fiction.   2. Haunted houses—Fiction.   3. Courage—Fiction.]
I. Munsinger, Lynn, ill.   II. Title.
PZ7.W7675Wj 1999   97-33308
[E]—dc21   CIP
                                                                                      AC

Typography by Elynn Cohen
1   2   3   4   5   6   7   8   9   10
❖
First Edition

I t was recess
at Teeny Tiny School.
Ghosts bumped
on teeny seesaws
and shrieked
on tiny swings.
The teeny tiny teacher
blew her whistle.

The timid
teeny tiny ghost
stood by
the slippery
silver slide.

"Come on up,"
called Cousin Brad.
"Slip and slide!
Ride and glide!"

Brad howled
and yeowled
as he slid.

"Your turn,"
said the teacher.
"Give a teeny tiny try."
With a shake
and a shiver
the teeny tiny ghost
flew to the
slippery tippy-top.

He shot to the bottom
and landed in a heap!
"You did it!"
cried his teacher.
"What a bold,
brave ghost!"

After school the teeny tiny ghost
soared above his teeny tiny town.
"Being brave just takes practice,"
he thought as he flew.

"Wait till I tell my black cats!"

But when he landed
at his teeny tiny house,

his back door was
standing open!

"Whooooooo's that prowling
in my teeny tiny house?"

he asked in a shiver-quiver voice.

He heard chains clinking
down his teeny tiny hall.
"*Whoooooooo's* there?"
he called.

Then the eyes of Great-Grampa
in the picture on the wall
began blink, blink, blinking—
open . . . shut!

The teeny tiny chair started

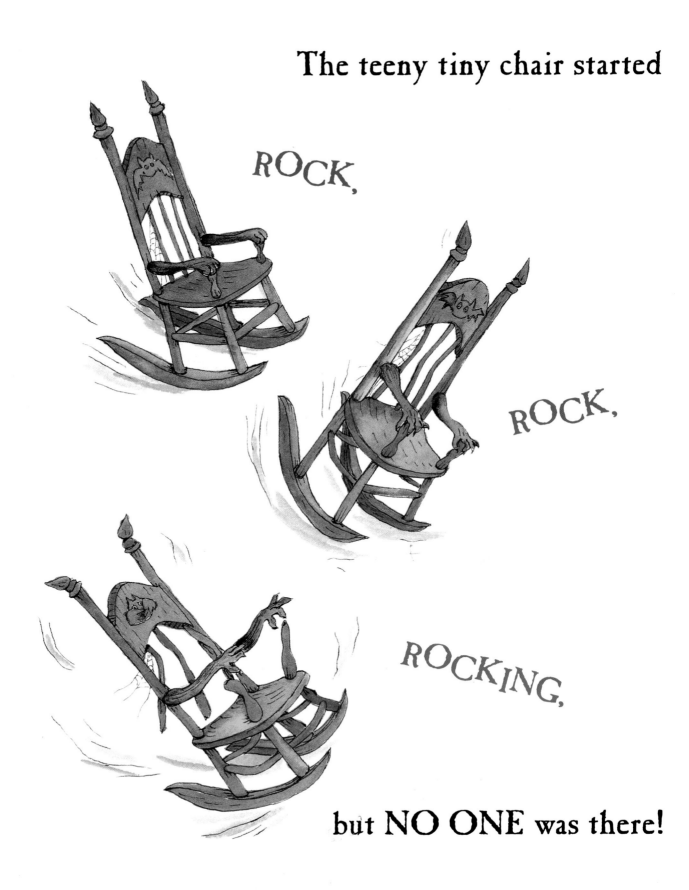

ROCK,

ROCK,

ROCKING,

but NO ONE was there!

"How can this be?"
he asked his teeny tiny cats.
"Someone is haunting
my teeny tiny house,
but *I'm* the ghost!"

Then came *stomp*,
stomp, *stomp*ing
on his teeny tiny stair.
"Where *are* you?"
he wailed,
his bright white face
turning pale.
But **NO ONE**
was there.

STOMP

STOMP

UMP

The teeny tiny ghost cried,
"What shall I do?
I learned *Booooooo*
and *Whooooooo*
at Teeny Tiny School,
but Hide and Haunt
isn't till next year!"

Then the teeny tiny ghost
remembered the slide.
How brave he had been
on that slippery, scary ride!

So he scooped up his cats,
and he sailed to his turret.

As he flew, he blew
out his teeny tiny chest.
"I am a brave, bold
teeny tiny ghost!"
he said as he
burst through
the door.

NO ONE was there.
He peeked
in his closet.
NO ONE was there.

Then the teeny tiny ghost
saw his teeny tiny curtains
blowing and flowing—
but there wasn't
any wind.

He zoomed
to his window
and gave a big yank!
With a thump
and a bump
his older cousin, Brad,
fell to the
teeny tiny floor.

"We had to hide and haunt
for homework,"
said Brad with a grin.
"I caught you!"
cried the teeny tiny ghost.

The cousins and the cats
danced the spook-and-spin.
Then they slid down
the teeny tiny rail.

They told rap-tap jokes and
made a marshmallow mess
till the time came
for Brad to go.

The teeny tiny ghost
waved a big goodbye
and whispered to his
teeny tiny cats,

"WAIT TILL NEXT YEAR!"